BETH ISRAEL

JOHN HEADX

First Published in November 2020

ISBN: 978-93-5427-016-1

BLUEROSE PUBLISHERS

www.bluerosepublishers.com

info@bluerosepublishers.com

+91 8882 898 898

Cover Design:

Joshua Freitas

Typographic Design:

Namrata Saini

Distributed by: BlueRose, Amazon, Flipkart, Shopclues

1

She came to me confused, indulging herself by telling me all these trivial things about her relationship with this young Greek man. She spent our entire encounter talking about that man and his relationship with her, and about his perspectives on nature and his surroundings. She wanted to talk to me about her Greek lover, and as I've always been beside her, a silent listener, I listened, suppressing my own feelings. I know that today's world demands that we listen to each other more and more, especially if the encounter happens in this small tavern, while she is indulging herself by looking at the young men around her, and as I've always been polite, clear and shy, I crushed my own feelings, my feelings that were urging me to subdue that girl, and her Greek lover if I had to. She knew, that I won't be able to resist her charm, even if it's the simplest blink of an eye, and I proved to her in each step, move, gesture and whisper, that I am willing to subdue her. I was in love, and she was in pride, and sometime I would be vulpine and she would silently come closer to me, wishing to cure me of my 40-day slumber I had with a lady, of whom all I know about was that she fought with me and subdued me effortlessly; her hand came down on the volcano of my claw. She was, without a doubt, a lady of the first exquisite nectar. But this one, an immigrant in Italy, of Libyan origin, had a Russian figure and overwhelmed me with the grace of her words, and restrained my needs, for, while I was like all lovers, a wild lion, her words came down on me like a bolt of lightning, 'So it is you!'

You figured me out!

Yes, it is you

I didn't give her an answer, showing her that I am lazy-looking and unthankful, a lover of pleasures, lost in the drink that brings together the child, the infant, the young, and the old; she was simply satisfying me. 'Is it you?' she asked.

'I don't know what you are talking about, ma'am!' I said.

"Is there anyone else here?!' she replied.

I looked around. Yes, I'm in the hospital, and he is my pretty doctor, and so I want to sit to the table to make more sense, but added another question:

'Is it you?'

'I don't know who am I, how I look like, not nothing of what you're saying!' I said, 'Who am I, gentlemen? Who am I?!'

'Seems you have lost your memory!' she said.

'What is "Memory"?' I asked her.

'What do you look like?' she asked.

'I had claws and teeth and some scars from the battled. I was born in the jungle; I haven't found anything about my history and who am I, or even what language I speak.'

'Do you have a family, a friend, or maybe a business, so that we can contact them?' she asked.

'What does a "friend" mean? I don't remember!' I said.

'How did you get into the hospital? she asked.

'I don't know!'

'What do you know about yourself?'

I looked around. I saw some men who seem to be the hospital's security staff handcuffed to that bed; everyone was anxious.

'Who are you?' she asked me again.

'I don't know!'

'Why do you refuse to take your medication?' she asked.

'What is the meaning of "medication"?' I asked, 'What is this place? I want to go back to the jungle I was born in!'

'You were sentenced by a judge to stay in this hospital until you get your memory back,' she explained, further questioning me, 'Do you know the name of this state and this country?'

'Senegal!' I answered.

'You are in the United States of America, in Massachusetts, in the city of Boston,' she said

I looked at her in wonder. 'So you say I'm not in Senegal!'

'No, you are in America' she replied, 'Do you know anything about America? Do you know the name of the American president? Have you been watching the television?'

'What is a "television"?!' I asked.

Do you recall storming into Brookline police quarters in Boston? You staged a protest inside the police quarters and disrupted the official police business there', she said, 'Do you remember any of this?'

'Are we in Senegal? I see some dark-skinned people holding things I can't recognize; I'm positive we're in Senegal with my own folks,' I said

'You carry a Saudi passport. Are you from Saudi Arabia? Do you remember who you are?' she asked.

'What is "Saudi Arabia"?', I wondered, 'This is the first time I've heard of this name! Is it a restaurant or a grocery store? Is it a piece of cake that I can eat?'

'So you don't know that you are in big trouble?' she asked me.

'Now, I know I'm in Senegal, and these dark-skinned folks around me are my people.'

'You are in serious trouble here!'

'I don't know who I am!'

'Are you a spy? What is the nature of your work?' she kept questioning me.

'I teach the Holy Quran to children in Senegal!' I insisted.

'Do you remember anything from Quran?' she asked.

'I don't know, but what I do remember clearly and haven't told anyone about it, is that my mother is Christian and my father is a Jew, and I was raised by a Muslim family,' I said

'What's the name of this family?'

'Nour Al Hak (the light of the right) in Senegal'

'Do you remember your full name ?'

'I don't know.'

'Repots say that you were homeless in the streets of Boston city, what did you use to do?' she asked me.

'Can I be in more than one place at the same time?' I asked instead.

'Do you know the name of this medical center?' she asked.

'What is its name?'

'Beth Israel Deaconess Medical Center of Boston city'

'What's today'sdate?'

'You have a strange condition. I have to prepare a report for the course about your case,' she said, 'and you will have to answer some of my questions later on.'

2

What have I put myself into? What is this fortified room? Why is the door like this? Why am I here? I only found an answer in the bed I am lying in, and the bag of nutritional serum injected into my hand. I moved around in Beth Israel Medical Center, pushing that serum around with me. I touched the walls; there's definitely something I don't understand! Who am I? Why are all these guards at the room's door? Why are all these looks surrounding the door's window? Who are you all?

He rushed towards me and asked 'Would you like a kosher meal? Do you eat pork and its products? Or would you prefer Jewish kosher meals that are in compliance with Islamic rules of Halal?'

'I'm not a Muslim!' I said.

'Who are you, then?' he asked.

'I'm a Jew' I replied.

'Kosher it is then.'

'I don't consume pork products, there's no problem. I was a Muslim once and a Christian, and now I'm a Jew. Is there a problem?' I demanded.

'I'll get you a kosher; you don't seem to go by the teachings of the religion,' he said.

'Then I'm an atheist.'

'What?'

'Have you worked with the US Army?'

'Yes, I worked with the US Special Forces in Baghdad,' he said

'Is this why you are rough with people? Do you know my name?'

'No, I don't know who you are!'

'Me neither!'

'We have piles of papers about the Israeli Mossad, the American CIA, Iraqi Intelligences, Saudi Intelligences and the Arab Spring. We have a treasure of information in these papers all under the title "Top-Secret". Do you remember any of these?' he asked me.

'I don't know anything of that', I replied, 'What's my name?'

'Do you want kosher?' he asked me instead.

'What is "kosher"?'

'Halal.'

'Where was it made?'

'I don't know'

'Am I a high risk and dangerous? For how long have I been in this high-risk-cases room?'

'A week.'

'What's today's date?'

'What do you think?'

'The last date I saw was 32-3-2033'

'We're not there yet!' he exclaimed.

'What is this place?'

'This is a place for psychiatric patients, and the room you're in is for the high-risk patients; a judge has ordered that you be put in here.'

'Can you help me join US Special Forces?'

'One of the conditions for joining the American army is that the applicant must be clear of posychiatric illnesses.'

'Then there's a problem!'

'You are in a big problem,' he agreed.

'What do you have in kosher today?'

'Shawarma and some soup.'

'Do you have any hotdogs?' I asked.

'We will give you kosher hotdog.;

'I don't want kosher, I just want some regular hotdog, with kosher Shawarma, and some pomegranate juice, if possible, with two scoops of chocolate and vanilla ice-cream.'

'I'll see what I can do,' he said, before adding, 'You really are in big trouble.'

3

'Wake up!'

I pulled myself together and opened my eyes, and there it was. Some falafel and appetizers like humus. He didn't bring the ice-cream I had asked for.

'Why didn't you bring me my ice-cream? And it's dinner time now, we don't eat falafel' I told the man.

'Who do you mean by "we"?' he asked.

I'"We" are inventers of falafel. I'm from Uzbekistan,' I answered him.

'And what does falafel have to do with Uzbekistan?'

'A cook from Israel travelled more than 2000 years ago to Uzbekistan, and there, he made the falafel.'

'This information is as confidential as the papers they got when they apprehended you red-handed at the police quarters.; he said.

'There's a conscience dilemma. Don't you know history?'

'It's true I'm dark-skinned, but I know that the main source of falafel is the streets of New York.'

‘Seems you have a great sense of security due to your service at the US Special Forces.’

‘I have seen many movies, but a person with a Saudi passport and claiming to be Jewish and suffering of memory loss... That’s a bunch of weird confidences!’

‘Who is the current president of America? Is he Netanyahu?’

‘Who is Netanyahu?’

‘Eliezer Netanyahu.’

‘His name is Benjamin Netanyahu.’

‘I don’t know any Benjamin Netanyahu, I said, ‘What I do know is that a lightyear ago, I opened the New York Times while I was in a space shuttle travelling out of the solar orbit with an internet connection and discovered that Benjamin Netanyahu is the new President of the United States. Haven’t you read the newspapers?’

‘You went there with NASA or with the Russians?’

‘Who is the Russian President now?’

‘I don’t know anyone in Russia, and I don’t know who their President is. Who do you think he is?’ he asked.

‘Once, when I was in Moscow watching the World Cup in 2018, when I was a young man, and this was many years ago, , their President was Yasser Arafat.’

He gave me a look, then seemed to keep a hold on himself, and called the security and the medics. They came and gave me a shot. I couldn’t help myself, I passed out and found myself, with the grace of good imagination, in those fascinating and lovely days with my Libyan mistress, together in London. I asked her in my dream, 'Have I seen you before?';Yes,' she replied, 'you have. I'm just a little jinni inside your cloths... wake up, wake up, wake up...' Saying this, she hugged me. I opened my eyes.

A security guard was holding my head and examining it!

'What are you doing?' I exclaimed.

'This device can examine your entire body. You told them you have a microchip planted in your body, so we had to be sure, he answered me calmly, and then suddenly screamed, 'Who are you?'

'I'm just a homeless man from the streets of Boston city,' I repllied, 'and I have the paper that proves that I'm homeless! What else do you want from me?'

'You are a Mossad for sure, aren't you? Who else knows about this but you?'

'Who am I? Answer me!' I demanded.

'At minimum assumption, you are an outlaw, and we must deal with you according to the regulation and rules.'

'Yes, I have worked with more than 20 intelligence agencies around the world, and my file is available at tables of all grand decision-makers in the world. I kicked the American army out of Iraq.'

'So you're saying you're not Mossad, but are in the American army?' he asked.

‘I don’t know anything about armies. Are you in the American army?’

‘ Yes, I work for the military intelligence in the US Army.’

‘I don’t know anything. I’m just a homeless man in the streets of Boston. Can you assign a lawyer for me?’

‘The court had already assigned one for you, but you refused to cooperate with him!’ he said.

‘We lacked intellectual conformity.’ I told him.

‘We’ll see what we can do for you.’

‘Can I have two scoops of chocolate and vanilla ice-cream?’ I asked him.

‘You are really in big trouble,’ he replied instead.

4

'Wake up. Your new lawyer is coming to see you.'

I couldn't help myself; I still hate lawyers.

'What's your name?' he asked.

'I don't know. I don't remember anything,' I told him.

'Everyone here is anxious about you. They all see different things about you, especially after what you have been accused of doing at the police quarters in Brookline, Boston,'

'What is "Brookline, Boston"?'

'One of the most luxurious residential neighborhoods in Boston City, where a lot of Jewish families live. You claim to be a Jew, but you're not, you're a Muslim, aren't you?' he asked me.

'I'm an atheist,' I replied.

'Yes.'

'Yes, I am an atheist from a Jewish dynasty; my father and mother are Jewish.;

'Which Jewish community do you belong to?' he inquired.

'Mizrahi.'

'You're a Mizrahi?'

'No, but a man at an African restaurant in Dorchester told me about my family's story and that we are Mizrahi,' I said. 'Do you want to go ask him? He can tell you about my family as he's the only one who knows.'

'Do you have his number?'

'You can find him sleeping in the streets, close to Northeastern University. You can find him there, tall, white, and speaks Japanese fluently.'

'We can't rely on him as a witness in any case. Is he a homeless like you?'

'Yes, he's my friend. He gives me cigarettes and we drink beer together in the streets; he knows me as a man of great wisdom with a heart of a lion,' I said.

'Do you know – at least – what your name is?'

'He said my name was Mohammed!'

'You're from a Jewish family, an atheist, you say, and your name is Mohammed?!'

'Do you have a problem with that?'

He stayed silent for a moment and then said, 'Soon many detectives and doctors from different intelligence and security agencies in the United States will be in this medical center, and you will be subjected to a lot of interrogations and close examinations.'

'Before all that,' I said, 'can you please get me two scoops of chocolate and vanilla ice-cream?'

'You are seriously in big trouble.'

5

'What's your name?' he asked.

'I don't know!' I replied.

'When did you lose your memory?'

'When I walked into the African restaurant, the man there told me about a dream he had. There was a kitten playing next to an ice-cream place in Dorchester. It was small and it brought to me a piece of banknote that goes back to the times of the Seljuk kings, and then I went to bed and saw her in front of me, that naughty devil.'

'Stop!'

'Is there a problem? Let me finish the story.'

'We didn't come here, doctors from the US military intelligence, to listen to you telling us a story about the African restaurant in Dorchester.'

'Do you know who am I?' I asked him.

'Yes. Do you have any relation to the emerging of the Internet, the major online websites, and other advancements in the 90s of the past century and the new millennium we living in now?'

'This is the first time I have ever heard of such a thing. Seems like my age allows me to write a secret report for the aliens about the projects I've worked on because they're the only ones who'd believe me,' I said, adding, 'Do you know who am I?'

'Are the masterminds behind the cutting of Internet cables in several locations?'

'I learned from the security staff here that you've worked with 20 secret service agencies around the world. Is this true?'

'I don't know what you're talking about, but one security guard told me that he's with the US Special Forces. Does he work for you? I don't know, but he's a good-hearted manI said. 'He got to me two scoops of falafel and Egyptian Tahini, with some appetizers and a lot of pistachios and a bit of wine or pomegranate juice.'

'Can you tell me the names of the 20 secret service agencies you've worked with?'

'Yes, I remember. These agencies work from inside the volcanos found at the bottom half of the Russian book "War and Peace", and some new ideas came to me, yes, I remember. I worked with US President Eliezer Netanyahu previously, and my good friend from the US Special Forces gave me a hotdog, no, he didn't... I think I really need to sit naked in front of you.'

'Here?' he asked incredulously.

'Why not? I replied. 'It's kind of an undisclosed physical liberation. Yes I'm wearing clothes that cover me now, but there are exposed parts of my body that urge me to do some yoga in front of you, and connect with the revelation through satellite and with other planets, so I can answer your questions. And you, lawyer! Why are you keeping your mouth shut? I said I'm Jewish and my name is Mohammed, what's wrong with you? Answer them!'

'You have nothing to do with the lawyer; we are here on unofficial basis,' he said.

'Here sits the lawyer, and is unofficially talking to me, but you're more than 20 people in here and I can't remember a thing you said, now, honestly, all I want is two scoops of chocolate and vanilla ice-cream.'

'What is your relation to the program "Eye of God"?'

'I don't what you're talking about.'

'Do you know who you are?'

'I don't know.'

'We know who you are.'

'Who? Me?'

'If I'm correct,' he said, smiling, 'and according the papers we have which were written by you when you were arrested by the Brookline PD and admitted to the medical center, I am, then it is you!'

'Who am I? Tell me please, my memory is way too crippled.'

'You *are* him!' he said, smiling.

I smiled back at him: '"Him" who?' I asked mockingly.

'You are one of the brightest minds ever in the US Military Intelligence Agency! Your name is widespread all over the world.'

'I don't know what you're talking about.'

'You must know something! Do you remember anything that can help us take an action? Anything at all?'

'"Him" who?' I smiled back mockingly at him.

'YOU!' he shouted nervously.

'Who? Me?'

'YOU ARE HIM!'

'Do you think I'm a legend?'

'You're bigger than all legends.'

'Yes, that man from the other restaurant in Dorchester told me, while he was grilling some Shish Kebab for me, that he was making this Shish Kebab especially for the "Legend of the American Homeless". I didn't believe him, though I'm a homeless myself in the streets of Boston.'

'And why did he say that?'

'Because I had told him in the past that I'm, as a homeless, can't buy humus form an American restaurant; I'm form Uzbekistan and I adore Humus.'

'And what does that have anything to do with Kebab, Marcos?'

'Who's Marcos?' I asked. 'Is it a new name of a new type of Italian Kebab-grilling designed for interactivity with the worldwide web?'

'Do you realize that I've always heard your name here and there, throughout my 20 years of service? Do you know who you are?'

'I don't know.'

'Do you want me to remind you of who you are?'

'I want two scoops of chocolate and vanilla ice-cream with some wine,' I said, 'if that is not possible, may I go down the block so I can buy myself a bottle of cheap wine? I used to look at this bottle from a distance all day long, salute it and hug the glass of the shop's window. May I?'

'You are here by the order of the court, and so you have to adhere to the treatment; with this attitude of yours, no one can help you, not me, nor anyone in the US government, the Department of Defense, Homeland Security, not even the CIA.' He suddenly changed the topic 'Do you know what does it mean to announce that you're alive? Well and sound here in the States? Do you know?'

'I don't know! I don't remember anything!'

'Do you remember anything about the early beginnings of the Internet private commercial business in the 90s of the past century?'

'Do you have a buck?'

'I do.'

'Go donate it to the Church of St. Mary in Brookline on a Sunday' I told him.

'Why?'

'Because the Bishop of St. Mary's church gave me shelter, somewhere to sleep at night, in one of the old churches of Boston.'

'Why are you doing this to yourself? You can gain billions if you just give straight answers to my questions!'

'You can ask that to your Marcos; as for me? I don't have answers for your questions!'

'You know, I served in Iraq, where everyone quietly and secretly mentions you name?'

'I don't know anything about what you're saying,' I said, 'seems you don't know who I am! I'm an average person, with no ambition; I love ice-cream, two scoops of chocolate and vanilla. I mastered the art of running from one place to another and I don't know anything. Do you want me to pray for you? Looks like you want me to talk to the doctors at Beth Israel medical center to get you a bed here, right next to me, so they can check your sanity and psychological wellness.'

'With your behavior? Apparently, we are all going to sleep in this hospital! Where are you going with all this, huh? Do you have another operation? Something new you want to do? Everyone knows about your multibillion US dollars' worth of accounts you have abroad; is it true?'

'And I have decided to let go of all this money and live a homeless life in the streets of Boston!'

'You have something to do here; Washington is concerned and they have no other way to handle you but violently. You are one of the fiercest fighters out there, and that is crystal-clear to me now.'

'Do you know when the new 100 dollar bill was printed?'

'When?'

"In the year 2070, I stumbled upon my poor neighbor who wanted to borrow a hundred bucks, so I gave a 100 dollar bill to him after I wrote on it, "You will give it back to me in 4066".'

'What US president was printed on the 100 dollar bill?'

'Saddam Husain.'

'Seems like we don't have any hope for today. What are you up to? I want to know. What thoughts do you have for the future?'

'I want you to talk to the chef of this hospital for me. Yes, I'm a Jew, but I don't each Kosher. I want to eat stake with some French fries and some dessert, and I want them to listen to me when I talk about the true history of the world, and when I talk about the American presidents, Eliezer Netanyahu and Saddam Husain, and I want them to get me a feminine fragrance from Kiev Mart, some wooden boxes and the tools required to manufacture beer, so that I can start working quietly in my detention room, or whatever you want to call it,' I said, adding. 'Do you want to know my name?'

'Yes,' he replied, 'I do.'

'Mustafa,' I said.

'Mustafa Khan?' he asked.

'Yes,' I said, 'now I remember, I had some Indian clothes called Raymond, yes, my name is Raymond.'

'So it's neither Mohammed nor Mustafa?' he asked.

'I don't know.'

'Looks like we have to leave. In case you want to talk, all you have to do is call your lawyer, who was appointed to you by the court, and we will come to you on unofficial basis. Seems there is no way around with you, is there!'

INext time you come, bring with you two scoops of chocolate and vanilla ice-cream, don't forget... what's your name?'

'Mark.'

'Frank?'

'Mark.'

'Am I in Heaven?'

'You are at Beth Israel Medical Center in Boston city.'

'Can you sense the importance of ice-cream while we're in heaven?'

'There's no ice-cream in heaven.'

'Are you an alien form outer-space, who has an ice-cream that is better than two scoops of chocolate and vanilla?'

'Yes, and with all respect, we're actually here to talk to you!'

'You're talking to Marcos, not me! I don't know any Marcos!'

He looked towards the lawyer and everyone else. 'Let's get out of here.'

Then hospital guards came and escorted me back to the room of high-risk patients.

6

Do you doubt me? Here, in this room which hates life, in this hospital and this section where the most aggressive security officers, military, and CIA come together! What is happening around me? What am I going through? How many days have I spent with them force medicating me? What is going on with me? Yes, I do have a furious past in dealing with the hardest torture equipments and their harshest and cruelest ones. Yes, I am a secret service agent, but I don't follow any country, city, or politics. I am free-contractor, or as they call me, "a mercenary".

I have lived my entire life dealing with intelligence agencies, my ideas, visions, dreams, strategies, and tactics are being taught in many places in the secret world; my companies and the empire I have built with my blood and sweat are now financing the biggest intelligence agencies in the world, and on top of them, the CIA. Do you want me to confess to all of that? The people of the United States, the great nation, will not believe the amount of information I have. The solution is not to confess my identity, the solution is to act like a psychopath, because what I have is not about money, glory, or position; it is science, history, geography, logic, civilizations, and the paradises of the entire world. There's no escape from it all.

This is the solution. Stay like a mental patient forever, if necessary, because this science and knowledge that I created will be badly abused by secret service agents if it is released into the White House and to the world of politics with no restraints; those who came to me have no big experience in dealing with politicians around the world.

We, as secret service agents and mercenaries, find difficulties in dealing with the politics that the White House issues and are imposed by the power of legitimacy and the laws controlled by untrained minds who are incapable of decision-making using the usual intelligence logic.

We disagree with those politicians in the White House and everywhere. There is no way out; men everywhere are asleep, and I'm here facing people who do not understand, and they don't possess the diverse sciences I have and huge fortune extended everywhere in the world.

The issue is not the money; the issue is that something on the top of the pile has been crippled, and we have to find a resolution. What is the solution now? Sleeping?

The solution is to let go of rationality, pretend to be insane and a psychopath, so that the days would lead us to that world in which you find paradise every time you close your eyes.

Here, I had to go on this road alone, as I've always done; they call me a mercenary though I'm into the for money, they call me mercenary because I neither work for the White House nor for any other intelligence agency in any country. They call me that so they can compromise me and make me a criminal in the eyes of the law, for they can take advantage of me when they need someone to break the laws they had previously made, for other benefits and purposes.

The solution now is to gather in paradise as it looks like the White House had lost everything, and if we keep following the same strategies in the Middle East where I live and everywhere else, then we are, no doubt, getting closer to a nuclear war. The solution is to act, and the right action now is the hibernation of intelligence activities, deactivation of any movement for any intelligence agency, and penetrating them to cripple the billions of dollars around the world, and moving by the name of laws and legitimacy.

It's time now for us comrades, to play according to laws and legitimacy, but how? We are not countries, governments, parliaments, or entities; we are security companies and financial empires, imposed out of necessity on the politicians, and it gave us a large space of movement in crises. So what is the solution? All this was floating around in my head, and a lot is floating around here and there, until the door of the room was opened.

;Are there two scoops of vanilla and chocolate ice-cream?' I called out.

'There's an injection,; the nurse who came in replied, 'do you want to take it? Or do you want me to call the guards outside your room to help me out? Based on what your serious mental condition requires...'

Since you didn't bring the two scoops of vanilla and chocolate ice-cream with you,' I interrupted her, 'please call for security to enforce me to take the injection'

She shouted out to the army and the military intelligence personnel, who came to help her give me the injection.

'There's no freedom,' I shouted out loudly, 'we are in the United States of America and I can't have two scoops of vanilla and chocolate ice-cream? It's the age of slavery, not freedom! The White House has lost their mind when they didn't give me the two scoops of vanilla and chocolate ice-cream! It's a matter of life and death! I can't be treated mentally if I don't have the two scoops of vanilla and chocolate ice-cream...' At this, they showered me with blows from all sides, fixed me to the bed in this gloomy room, and gave me the prescribed injection.

They were about to leave when I called out, 'I want to have my entire rights; where is the vanilla and chocolate ice-cream? You are in the age of slavery!', adding, 'Your military training is a failure, and you are such losers.'

They left the room, so I told myself it seems like no ice-cream will be coming, so I must ask for a cold glass of beer and some appetizers instead.

I smiled a little to myself and said, 'It seems they insist that I either subdue and confess with what I know, or I stay described as insane everywhere. Here, I knew the solution; to stay under the cover of insanity until further notification, ruled by all necessities of geography, history, politics, logic, and all what the newly developed work needs require.

I sang a few songs I had memorized, and then shouted out to the guards with the military background in the American Army and its intelligence, 'Do you have a radio around here?'

Someone came to me and said, 'There's a radio. It's like a headphone, you put them in your ears, but you're going to hurt yourself, aren't you?'

'Of course not,' I said, 'after you gave me that injection, and after your civilized behavior towards me, I feel much better, so now I want some music so that I can calm myself down a little.'

'It sounds like you are kidding with me,' he said, 'I've read your entire file. You are different than all the people I've met in my whole life.'

'Bring me the radio, I said, 'and I'll commit to the treatment plan. I respect the law. I came to America to study law. And don't forget the two scoops of vanilla and chocolate ice-cream.'

'I'll see what I can do,' he said and then left. The nurse came in with a lot of warnings and threats that

I have to stay calm, I am not to shout, and I'm not permitted to have any radio or anything else. I have to obey everything she tells me to do, else the security officers from different military and intelligence agencies will deal with me. Then she left with her threats I had gotten used to listening to since I had come to this place.

7

They stormed into the room in Beth Israel Medical Center. Their looks were intense. *It's a new delegation of those trainers, the Congress and White House bootlickers,* I said to myself, *it's a problem with them as usual.* 'Who are you people?' I asked them.

'Don't talk.' he said. 'We do the speaking here. You will remain silent.'

'I want two scoops of vanilla and chocolate ice-cream,' I said.

'What were you doing in the Kingdom of Saudi Arabia?'

'I was working in movie shooting, and wrote articles on politics and news.'

'Details.'

'First, I worked with a charity society for the teaching of Quran memorizing; then I worked as a news reporter for more than one channel. I also participated in designing media strategies for more than a media body around the world. I contributed, as well, in designing military defense formations in more than a place around the world', I said, adding, 'But all that wasn't in Saudi Arabia, it was – if I recall correctly – in Israel, precisely in Yafa, where I was running a big team of scientists under the headline of – and here I said it in plain Arabic language – "The shy don't live long".'

'So you speak Arabic?'

'The shy don't live long is in the Assyrian language. My Jewish grandfathers used to speak it, those who learned the Holy Quran, memorized it and change their religion after the era of Jamal Abdel Naser, and then traveled to Jerusalem to serve humanity and save minds.'

'Then you are Jewish?'

'No, I'm a monotheist Muslim.'

'You haven't prayed even once since you got into the hospital.'

'My Islamic religion obliges me to keep my worships private. I don't pray in front of British intelligence agents.'

'I'm not British. That's rude.'

'It sounds you are a Muslim. Then let's pray together to thank God for our reunion here in this holy place.'

'Sounds like you are an atheist.'

'I have my memory back! I'm a Soviet, I was trained by USSR and received my orders just before it collapsed; my orders were to penetrate the White House, and I'm here to execute and operation inside the mind of the US President, Eliezer Netanyahu.'

‘In what year did you receive your training?’

‘I was trained in 3099, while I was inside my mother’s womb in the jungle with monkeys, mules, and donkeys’

‘You are in big trouble,’ he said.

‘We come from two different schools; you were trained to follow orders, while I was trained to discard them. We could never come along.’

‘Is there anyone you know in Saudi Arabia, Pakistan, or Afghanistan, who can help us with your identity? If you reveal your identity yourself, or even tell us what secret service agency trained you, we won’t have any problem with you. Your stubbornness and arrogance, and you claiming insanity is what confuses us; your file at all the agencies around the world speaks a great deal about you; we have learned a lot from you.’

‘Then I’m in big trouble!’

‘Why?’

‘You and all the people of intelligence at several agencies don’t know exactly, till now, who am I; you all think I’m interested in proving who I am to you? I’m not me! And this is enough for dealing with you people for now.’

'You are not you, that’s one thing we all know, but you have to prove it to us.’

‘This is enough for dealing with you for now, and for the future, according to the needs of the moment, and the followed strategies and tactics, and upon that you have to agree.

'I accept, but others at the White House, the Congress, the US Armey, and all the American secret service agencies will not accept.'

'I don't care.'

He remained silent for a moment, and then asked, 'Is it true that you have a microchip implanted in your brain and had it linked to Google?'

'What?!'

'That's what everyone is talking about in secret,' he said. 'We all know who you are, why are you so stubborn?'

'What is "Google"? This is the first time I am hearing this name!'

'Your history is a proven record of your completion of this operation. You were behind it, and you truly are what they always say about you everywhere.'

'There has been a huge misunderstanding here; I used to be a baker in India, and if you lived there, you would've known my struggle with dough, even though I know nothing of what you're talking about. I don't use computers, and I don't know anything about them. All I know is that I'm a simple man, a baker. Yes, I remember, I used to work in selling shoes and then would beat people up with them. People from all over the world would come to me and would pay me money to buy shoes from me and then would let me beat them up with these same shoes.'

'We all know that you're the one who did it to him.'

'Who are you talking about?'

'To the American president...' He stopped talking then and smiled.

'There seems to be a big misunderstanding,' I said, 'and you seem to be imagining things that have never existed. I think I have to call the nurse in here immediately to give your sanity a quick check-up.'

'I'll leave now, but whatever it is that you're up to, you have to inform us. Never deal with it the way you do; every time you do something first, and then enforce everyone to comply with what you do.'

'You are free to leave, or you can stay and let me tell you again my story in the world of shoes.'

'There seems to be no solution here. I told you, you shall never impose upon us anything new. What's happening is very dangerous, and we can't tolerate all what you're doing here and there.'

'I want two scoops of vanilla and chocolate ice-cream.'

'This is a useless conversation.' He then left and closed door behind him. I sat in the room, surrounded by fortified walls, and this one small window that lets the sunlight sneak in onto the top of the wall. They seem to have really lost their nerves. They don't want to adhere to anything; they want to waste time. They want to know what will happen, they need some time off, and intensive mental treatment. They need hearing sessions at the Congress. They need a presidential administration that is aware of the magnitude of the risks resulting from the American and International composition. They need many things, and I can't expose anything now. Yes, they are security officers and secret service agents; one of the golden bases for us in our work is "The level of knowledge and its art correspond to the level of intelligence and political needs".

8

I started assessing the situation rapidly: I'm now in this room, surrounded by all these people. I really need to make a move now and call a friend in the Syrian Ministry of Foreign Affairs, so a diplomatic delegation would come over and pick me out of this mess. Is this the only way out? Yes, I don't want to reveal my identity. What should I do? There's so much to hide, the upcoming days has so much to hide for me, I have to move, I can't call anyone at the Saudi Embassy, nor the British Embassy. I can't call anyone else.

What I have to do is hurry up and call my old friends; for me, Syrian is Russia, and this is the solution to break this siege.

I have to get a phone and make this call. If I stay without a clear and obvious diplomatic backup, I'd never find a way out of this; they want the money, and they want to work with me, but I can't let them work with me. The current US president is influenced by his own emotions and desires when it comes to making any decision, especially those related to intelligence people inside the States. The solution simply is getting the help of old friends; in Arabic, Syria and Russia share the exact same letters, and for me, they are the same; it this point the yarn to old-school methods among intelligence people. Therefore, I have to move.

I can't visit my home, Saudi Arabia, not even the Arabia Gulf; if I do, the undercover agents of the American president and others will hunt me; the solution is to go far away from Saudi Arabia. There is no other possible solution, and I can't disclose the complicated covert operations that are taking place now everywhere, in the Middle East, Europe, and all over the world; so, the solution is to leave the Sates and Saudi Arabia and immigrate as far as possible until things settle down, because everyone is watching, observing, and analyzing , and I have too much to expose but no, not now, not in the time of this US president, who was described by the President of Philippines as "Son of a Bitch", and was treated so rudely in the People's Republic of China during the G20 summit, where all diplomatic practices where discarded. They didn't even bring him stairs for his jet when he arrived, and he had to go through the emergency exit. They didn't lay down a red carpet for him. This is how China is, big with its stance. Yes, everyone wants to treat this US President this way, everyone is waiting for the "Go" signal to leave the fruitless policies and strategies of this president; yes, he has to be dealt with anyway.

'Can I make a phone call?' I asked. 'I just remembered the number of a person who knows me and lived with me. He knows my name and address, he knows everything about me.'

'You're always like this,' he said, 'you're going to escape then!'

'This is his number, and I think he's ready.'

'Is he an Israeli?'

;No, from Syria.'

'As usual, keeping too many things to yourself.'

'Are you ready to take his number and call him, ask him yourself, and ask the social worker, the doctor, and everyone else to prepare all the reports they need to prepare?'

'What do you want us to tell him?'

'Are we talking off-the-record here?'

'Yes, speak!'

'"The man with the red bag filled with imported cheese, our old friend, is here in Boston", this is what I remember, and he for sure will know me,' I said.

'The red bag carried by the US Secretary of State, while he stepped down the stairs of a Russian airport to meet president Vladimir Putin; I recall the Russian president joking with the US Secretary of State about the red bag during their meeting at the Kremlin. The news casts kept showing how the Russian president joked about the red bag, saying the US Secretary of State has come in with a big bribe in the back.'

'I don't know what you're talking about.'

'I will make the phone call, but do you give me your word that you will return to the States when the term of current president, or the next one, is over?'

'Apparently, I lost parts of my memory, but that doesn't matter. I will come back one day, but I don't think I'm in the Boston city of America. I think I'm in Saudi Arabia, in a tent in the middle of the desert, are you ready for the call?'

'Yes.'

9

'My brother,' he said, 'Edward Marcos, thank God they called me!' He looked at them. 'You don't who this is? He is my half-brother.' He looked at me. 'You can't be here; you have to leave at once.'

He looked at them. 'May I make a phone call here?'

She said, 'He can't leave until the judge comes here tomorrow, and you tell the judge what you know.'

'Ok, I'm ready,' he said.

'Are you Syrian?' she asked.

'No,' he said, 'I'm an American citizen, but my brother has a European nationality.'

'You have to bring photocopies of his passport, and documents to prove he's not homeless, and he has an acceptable regular income, so we can present them to the judge,' she said.

'We have health testimony from an EU country, proving he suffers from several illnesses, including psychopathy.'

'You have to bring everything before the judge tomorrow.'

'I'll speak to my brother's lawyer so he'd come as well.'

'Tomorrow the court will take place here; he is a true brother, but a pain in the neck, and attracts a lot of attention, and you know what I mean by that.'

'I will help him as much as I can, in all possible ways,' he told her.

'So let it be,' I said.

10

The judge came to the medical center; the court convened inside the specialized division at Beth Israel Medical Center, and after the argumentation of my lawyer, and after the judge hailed me with countless questions, he ordered my release after my lawyer told him that I will be admitted back to the European hospital that was originally handling my advanced case of psychopathy; there, I will continue my treatment.

The lawyer added, 'We are aware of his condition, and we are ready for all financial compensations, and settle any financial dues for Beth Israel; we have spoken to the European hospital, and they are ready to accommodate him; they have sent his assigned nurse and she arrived today. She will escort him with us to the hospital in Europe.'

After all reassurances and medical reports presented by my half-brother, the judged ordered my release; the doctor prepared all requirements, and I left the States on the same day, and arrived at a European country early next morning.

www.ingramcontent.com/pod-product-compliance
Ingram Content Group UK Ltd.
Pitfield, Milton Keynes, MK11 3LW, UK
UKHW042001190726
13854UKWH00005B/2106

9 789354 270161